First published in the United States 1990 by Chronicle Books.
Copyright © 1989 by Ravensburger Buchverlag Otto Maier GmbH, West Germany
All rights reserved.
Printed in Hong Kong.   Japan.   Singapore.

Editor's Note: Younger children should only undertake these
projects under adult supervision. Parents and teachers should
match crafts to the appropriate skill level of the child.

Library of Congress Cataloging-in-Publication Data

Lohf, Sabine.
  [Ich mach was mit Steinen. English]
  Things I can make with stones / Sabine Lohf.
      p.   cm.
  Translation of: Ich mach was mit Steinen.
  Summary: Provides instructions for various rock craft
projects, including stone games, aquariums, stone castles,
and mosaic boxes.
  ISBN 0-87701-769-7
  1. Rock craft—Juvenile literature. [1. Rock craft. 2. Handi-
craft.] 1. Title
TT293.L64   1990
745.58'4—dc20   90-31935
                                             CIP
                                             AC

10 9 8 7 6 5 4 3 2 1

Chronicle Books
275 Fifth Street
San Francisco, California 94103

Things I Can Make with STONES

Sabine Lohf

You can make all these things with stones.

Chronicle Books • San Francisco

Collecting Stones

Stone Animals

Using clay, you can make these wonderful stone animals.

Hello, goat!

Mazes

You can even draw
a picture with stones.

Can you find
your way through the maze?

A small box
can make a
comfortable bed.

You and your friends can hunt for buried
treasure! Hide the golden stones and see
who finds the most!

Painted Stones

You can paint letters on stones and spell your name.

You are going to have a lovely red cap!

Stone Castles

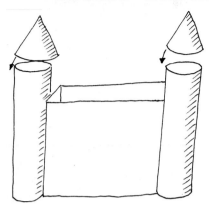

Glue paper towel tubes to the sides of a box. Then, spread plaster all over your castle and press the stones into the wet plaster.

Stone Cities

You can create a whole city out of painted stones or pieces of brick.

Racing Ladybugs

Place a smooth piece of
cardboard or paper on a slope.
Each racer chooses a ladybug
and places it at the top of the
slope, in its own lane. The one
who slides to the farthest end
first, wins!

Come on! Faster!

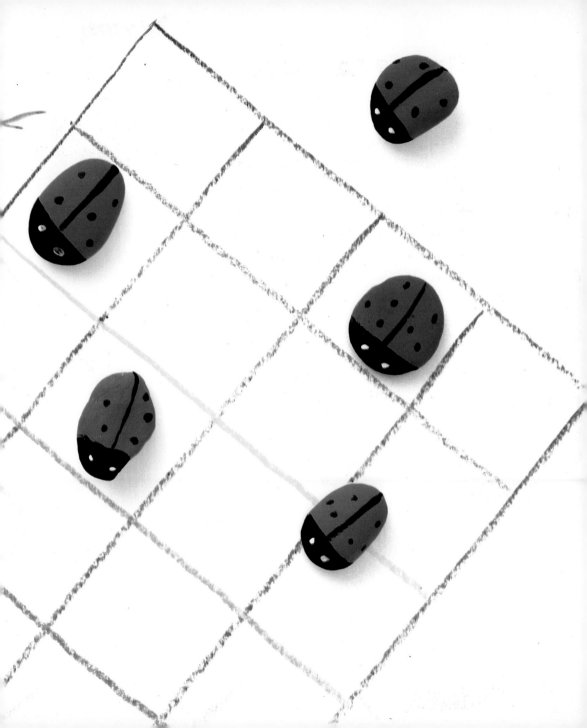

Aquariums

Would you like
to meet
some other fish?

A Stone Family

If you use your imagination, you can make all kinds of figures.

The little stone baby should sleep soundly now.

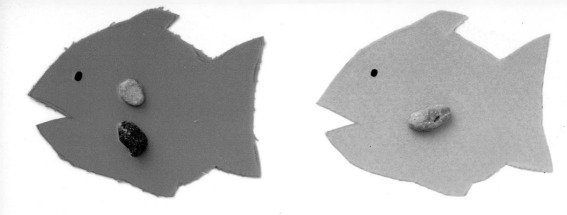

Stone Games

First, cut several fish out of colored paper, or with chalk draw them on a large piece of cardboard or directly onto the pavement. Each player takes a turn, aiming to land the stone on a fish. The player who gets the most, wins!

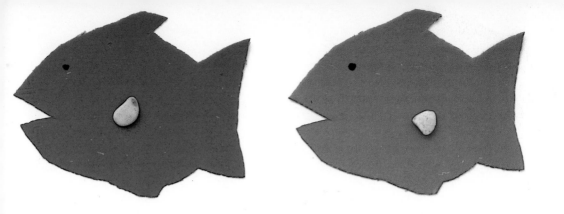

If you want an even more challenging game, paint the stones the same colors as the fish and try to land the stones on their matching fish.

Mosaic Boxes

Boxes make wonderful gifts.

I'll put this inside the box, too!